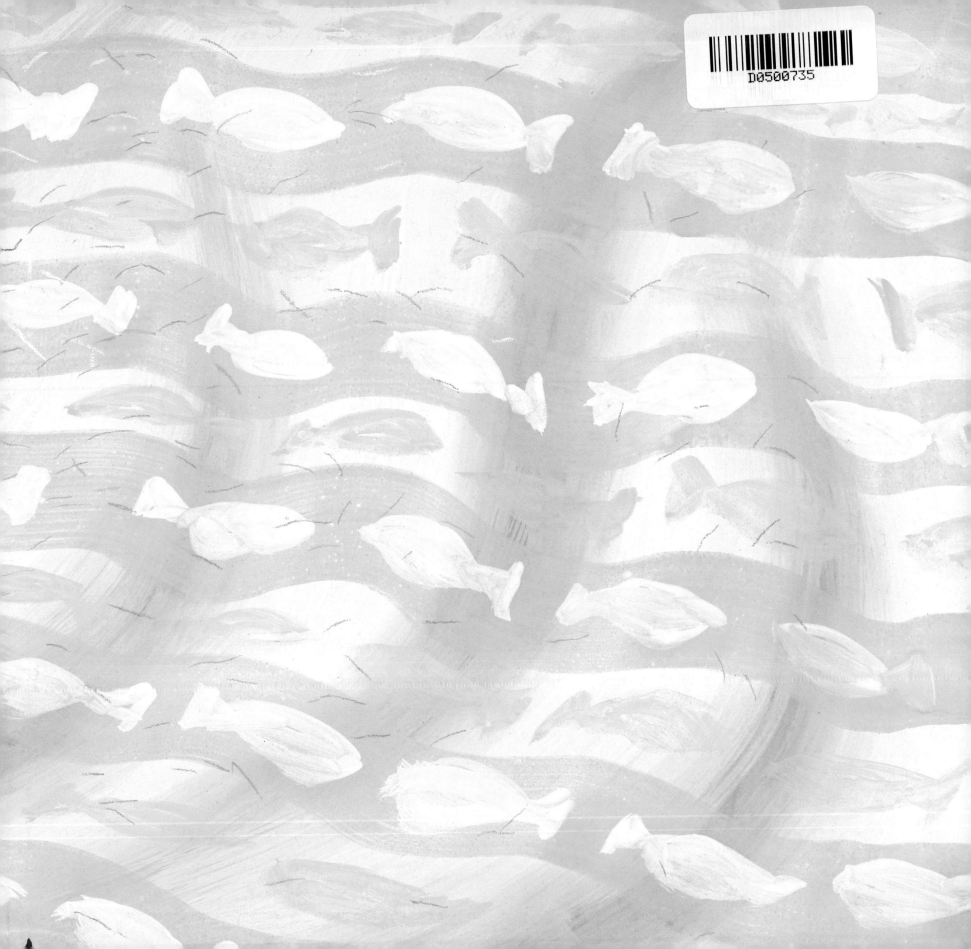

The Cat Who Liked Potato Soup

THE CAT WHO LIKED POTATO SOUP

Terry Farish

illustrated by Barry Root

CANDLEWICK PRESS
CAMBRIDGE, MASSACHUSETTS

There was an old man, an ol' Texas boy,
country-raised, don't you know.
Grew up hardy on fried chicken
and biscuits big as Lewisville Lake,
and with an army of cats
so as one looked about the same as another.
The old man couldn't count how many
had come and gone.

Now the place was wizened down
to the old man and one cat—
who he liked,
but not so's you'd notice.

The man and the cat lived
on a road called Chatterpie
for the string of blackbirds
who perched on the telephone wire.
The birds kept up a terrible ruckus.

"Make a good pie," the man said to the cat.
The cat licked her lips.
"Hogwash," the old man answered.
"How would you know how
them birds taste? You never killed nothin'."
Which was true, not a mouse, nothing.

The cat was fond of the man's potato soup,
which made him love her a breath more,
but not so's you'd notice.

The man and the cat had a pickup truck
and together they often rode
down to the lake to go fishing.

The cat sat on the bow of the boat,
her face into the wind,
like she was a hood ornament.

The man caught freshwater bass,
which were usually so small he kissed them
to wish them another season's growing
and tossed them back. The cat never caught nothin'.

One winter day,
the man hauled home
an electric blanket.
The cat looked at it as if to say,
"Well, finally."

The man knew what she said and he said,
"Aren't you uppity, Your Royalty."

The cat merely blinked,
then turned her gaze to the winter wheat.

The next evening the cat didn't feel
like rousing herself.
She wanted her food delivered.
The old man whispered, "Fool cat.
You ain't nobody's prize.
Never killed nothin'."

He brought her
a bowl of potato soup
on a small tray.

In the morning,
it was their time to go fishing.
The old man paused at the door,
pulled down the bill of his cap, said,
"You know, them fish don't wait on ya."
He said it slow. Give the cat a chance
to ramble out to the truck.
Nothing.
The cat took the deep,
deep breaths of a long sleep.

The old man shook his head.
He'd go. He'd go alone.
Who needed a cat?
Nothing but a bony cat.
Wouldn't even go fishing.

Alone, the old man launched his boat,
though the dawn held a heavy winter fog.
The boat just didn't handle.
The fish didn't bite.

At home, the cat's eyes opened.
No clatter in the kitchen. She waited.
He'd never left without her.

In the winter dawn, when the fog lifted
and the outline of the moon
remained in the sky, the cat waited.

Morning came.
The moon faded.
No soup. No old man.

The cat slipped off the bed and to the window
that they always left cracked.
Through this, she disappeared
into the flat, yellowed field.

When the old man came home,
he didn't find the cat lolling on the bed.
He looked in all his rooms. He had three.
She was not lolling in any of them.
She did not come home for lunch.
She did not come home for supper.

In the dawn there was still no cat.

The old man got up to go fishing.
He went fishing the next morning,
and the next.

Each time, he came home to an empty house.

"What's done is done,"
  he told himself one morning.
"I done right by a worthless cat
  that never caught nothin'."

He drove up the road called Chatterpie.
He drove up his and the cat's
dirt driveway. He walked, head down,
with a sorrowful face, until he came
to the front porch.

There was the cat—and
under her paw was a fish.
The fish did not require kissing
as it had had several seasons of prosperity.

The cat's eyes sparked with anger.
Her tail flailed and came down
in long, hard thumps on the creaky wood.
She glared at the old man.

The old man swept off his cap.
He stared at the cat.
He stared at the fish.
Even the birds hushed up at such a sight.
The cat did not care. Her eyes dared him
to touch that fish.

She would not talk, only howl.
She opened her mouth and howled
for a long time. The old man
had trouble making out the details
of her story, but she had swum and swum
and detested being wet.
And then there was the fish part.

He sat with her on the porch
until she was tired of telling him
how awful it had all been.
The story was very muddled,
but he was impressed.
It broke his heart.

She washed her ears until they stood up
and she looked more like herself.
The old man promised to take her with him,
no matter how bad she looked.
He had only thought she was maybe
too old for fishing.
She said she was sleeping!
Hadn't she earned a winter sleep?

He thanked her for the fish, which
of course she had not given him.
He told her never mind about
killing them birds or nothin'.
She was good enough like she was.
A little skinny, he added.

She ignored him.

The man made a new pot of potato soup
that night and he whistled.
The cat made a nest on the electric
blanket and she purred.

And he loved the sight of her, oh,
and this time you'd notice.
She was a little tender, though, and
refused to share the blanket with him—

until, in the night, a sliver moon
appeared in the sky and then came
sweet peace.

In memory of Jimmy Fowler of Combe, Oxfordshire
T. F.

To Benjamin
B. R.

First edition 2003

Library of Congress Cataloging-in-Publication Data

Farish, Terry.
The cat who liked potato soup / Terry Farish ; illustrated by Barry Root. —1st ed.
p.   cm.
Summary: The friendship between an old man and his cat, both of whom like potato soup,
is strained after he goes fishing without her.
ISBN 0-7636-0834-3
[1. Cats—Fiction. 2. Pets—Fiction. 3. Friendship—Fiction.
4. Fishing—Fiction. 5. Soups—Fiction. 6. Texas—Fiction.] I. Root, Barry, ill. II. Title.
PZ7.F22713 Cat 2003
[E]—dc21   2001043533

2 4 6 8 10 9 7 5 3 1

Printed in Italy

This book was typeset in OPTICather.
The illustrations were done in watercolor and gouache.

Candlewick Press
2067 Massachusetts Avenue
Cambridge, Massachusetts 02140

visit us at www.candlewick.com